READ BOOK 2 : 'HER' INTUITION

Please be sure to read the Book 2 in the series first, as there will be little to no recap of events thus far. To have the best experience possible, please read the previous title.

CHRISTOPHER

BLYTHE BARTRAM

HER REPUTATION

SHE KNOWS BOOK 3

ISBN: 0692937617
ISBN-13: 978-0692937617

CONTENTS

ACKNOWLEDGMENTS

Madeline E. Buhr / The Editor

Andrew Hess

Andrew graphics/Designer

SelfPubBookCovers.com/andrewgraphics

INTRODUCTION

Did you hear about that woman who was married to the King of England? They say she was in an incestuous relationship with her brother.

Well, surely you've heard of the Queen who wanted to cut off everyone's heads. I heard she was *all heart*. –What's that? You haven't heard?

Well, I'm sure you've heard about old "Georgie", King of England, mad as any man I ever did see. An entire country was led by a man who didn't even know what day it was, let alone his own name. Perhaps that one was past your time; it was only 1776 after all.

So, do you remember the guy who was absolutely hated in the First World War? He was tough as nails, but still united the country. He came to lead during the Second World War. They say he drank and smoked cigars nonstop. He was a tough old bastard though.

How about that Martin guy? He was way ahead of his time, they say. My friend swears he met him. He kept going on about this dream he had, like he was the only one to ever have a dream. What made him so special?

They were Anne Boleyn, the Queen of Hearts from Alice in Wonderland, King George III, Winston Churchill, and last, but by no means least, Martin Luther King Jr.

We all know that what we do or don't do, what we say or don't say, can all leave an imprint of us behind. We are not in control of our reputations. One's reputation is a culmination of other people's opinions, while all you can do is just sit back and watch it happen.

Women are no exception. Some women protest at "slut shaming" because they hope no one calls or thinks of them as a slut out of mutual respect. However, a woman's 'inner slut' is just as strong. Oh yes, there is such a thing. Every woman has one whether they know it or not, or if they're willing to admit it.

If *she knows*, then she will know how to shape your impression of her. If she wants to, she can appear innocent, weak, strong, dumb, intelligent. She can also appear flirtatious, if the situation warrants it, or the complete opposite. All she would need to do is mold her personality to the situation like an actress.

Even though one's reputation is created from the perspective of others, and we cannot directly control other people's minds, she can influence their perspective, thereby controlling her reputation.

I mean, *she knows* you want to be her white knight, to rescue the damsel in distress. So, why not play to that role? Having a strong protector does wonders. *She knows* to be seen as equal, she has to work twice as hard in this day and age to prove she is as capable as any man.

Reputations can be shaped and molded into finely polished weapons if done properly. Don't know how? *She knows.*

2 CHAPTER TWO

"X marks the spot." The term suits Norwich's International Airport in Norfolk, England remarkably well. It has two main runways which form a giant X while flying overhead.

This airport is nothing like its neighbors to the southwest, Heathrow and Gatrick. While the airport's name boasts international importance, it is actually a quaint little airport. Anyone living in America would assume it was just used for small local planes and those wishing to learn to fly.

Most of the flights travel out to Amsterdam, then on towards America, even though it is capable of sending out flights straight to New York City and back. However, the former of the two is more common, as the planes that fly in and out are owned by KLM, the Royal Dutch Airlines, or Koninklijke Luchtvaart Maatschappij, in the Dutch native tongue.

With the terminal only being one level, the passengers are required to walk out to their planes and vice versa, as if it was still the 1930s. It has its charm about it; it's like mixing the modern with the old.

As the sun shined bright, one would think it was scorching hot outside. However, the English wind gusts from the channel kept it a chilly summer's day. England: the only place where one could get a sun tan and shiver all at the same time.

One of the city's busses pulled up to the drop off point. The driver opened the door and exited the bus to open the luggage doors on the bottom of the bus. Raven and Chris exited the bus amidst the crowd of people. Chris had Raven's carry-on situated on his back with the straps over his shoulder.

Raven was sporting her signature black fedora hat. It was one of the few items she managed to keep hidden from her father and his woman friend. She also wore her thick black framed glasses, black lady slacks, and a low-cut navy blue and white stripe tank top, with a royal blue throw in hand. There was nothing to clingy, perfect for traveling.

Chris retrieved Raven's luggage from the driver, set it down on the ground, extended the handle, and began to roll it along behind them.

"Are you going to come to tell me just how you won this holiday for me?" Raven asked Chris, as they started to walk into the terminal.

"In a moment. Need to get you checked in," Chris responded, as he made his way to the check-in area with Raven following along behind him. He laid her paperwork on the desk, then took a step back, allowing Raven to step forward to answer questions for the check-in process.

Chris lifted Raven's luggage onto the conveyor belt for it to be weighed and tagged by the airline staff member behind the counter. Voices echoed all throughout the terminal. Although there were some other people around that had also arrived on the busses, there was an inescapable impression that the terminal was nearly empty.

Once Raven received her boarding pass, she and Chris headed over to a mini British Home Stores (BHS) outlet. Next to it was Boots, selling books, magazines, and newspapers from all across the world.

The main BHS store in the city center hosts a sit-down restaurant and small snack shop, which also supplies its counterpart in the airport. Chris ordered a breakfast roll, which was just two cooked sausages inside a kaiser roll, and Raven ordered an Italian sub sandwich. They went to sit down at one of the few tables that were provided for the airport's passenger's waiting to embark.

"I know you love the rock group, HIM. I saw online a chance to enter a contest and the question was really easy, so I entered," Chris started to explain.

"Right, so this hasn't anything to do with me?" she inquired, sounding skeptical.

"Well…" Chris started to reply, shifting in his seat. "It did. I mean, I know I can't help you. You don't want any help, so I am not. However, I knew you needed a break to get away. I entered never expecting to win. I mean, I'm sure thousands entered; however, I got lucky and I won you a ticket for HIM with backstage pass."–he held up the envelope containing the tickets and placed it on the table–"I'm keeping my word. I felt it wouldn't hurt you to go away for a short weekend or something."

"The prize was only the tickets, so how you get the plane ticket for me?" she asked next.

"I, erm… I asked an old friend who I know is in New York City. They found a good hotel for you and promised to look after you," Chris mustered.

"So, you asked your old crush for help," she stated sternly.

"What? How do you know?" he remarked with a surprised tone.

"You have the same dumb look on your face you had for years following her around. The same look you have anytime her name is brought up. You still love her, don't you?" she questioned, with an accusing look.

"No, I love you. It's been four years since I've seen her or heard from her. If anything, I wanted to know you were safe over there. I knew she went to New York, so I asked her to show you around. Just remember you are my first, not her," Chris explained.

"So, you did all of this for me?" she replied.

"Look, I'm not trying to help you. I know you love your sisters. I did this because I know you love their music and I know you always wanted to go see one of their performances. So, I saw the chance and I never expected anything from it, such a long shot. I can see you are stressed out and you needed a holiday more than anyone I know. So please believe me, I love you and there is no ulterior motive here other than to give you a holiday, so you can have some fun."–Chris reached down, pulled out a sealed envelope, and handed it to Raven–"Another to add to your collection when you get back, another letter. I thought you can read it when you are on the plane, if you find time."

"But you hate writing; you keep saying you are not good at it," Raven remarked, as she took the letter from him.

"I do, but I love you more than my hate of writing, so it should just show you how much you mean to me and why I did this for you." He stood up as Raven's flight was being announced over the intercom.

"Because you love me, and I love you too." She hugged him tight and kissed him. Then she proceeded through the door leading her to the outside toward the plane.

There wasn't any security to go through here. Since the flight was just headed to Amsterdam, it was considered an internal flight. At least until BREXIT came into effect, that is. From there, the flight would head out to New York.

Chris walked over to the 'observation deck,' which more accurately, was just a giant observation window. It allowed people to see out onto the air field. One could see the planes stationed outside with the motorized ladders leading up to the plane's entry door.

Raven headed straight out toward the ladder leading up to the plane. She wanted to look back, but tried to fight the urge. One of the many quotes Chris often recited came to her mind. *Never look back. Keep looking forward and obtain your goal. Looking back only distracts you.* When she reached the bottom of the steps, she couldn't fight the urge anymore and looked back towards the terminal.

"She loves me," Chris mumbled under his breath, as he smiled and waved to Raven. He waited until Raven was up and out of sight before he pulled out his cellphone. He opened up Facebook and started a quick message to Courtney, Lynn's friend from New York. Chris never actually got to speak to her in person, but only via Facebook. He had attempted to message Lynn; however, it was Courtney who answered initially, and she had been communicating for Lynn ever since.

She is on the plane on time. It's taxiing to the runway now. It will be in JFK in 10 hours.

Chris turned and looked around while waiting for a response about what he would be doing next. He didn't have to wait long, as he had only gotten about half way to the terminal's exit when the green light on his phone started to flash.

Understood. We are getting makeovers by Lynn's boss. I bet you won't even recognize her. Lynn will be touching down at 07:50 at NWI.

Chris exited the terminal and waited for the next bus to arrive to take him home until his scheduled return.

3 CHAPTER THREE

A red Dodge pulled into a parking spot outside the Presbyterian Hospital in Queens, New York. Lynn turned off the engine and grabbed her purse. She was wearing Hayden Loose Fit Boyfriend Jeans with a black lace tank top under a denim jacket. The entire outfit came from her favorite store, Topshop.

Lynn exited the car and locked it manually using the key, rather than with the wireless function of the remote fob. There was a breeze in the air, but it was still a warm New York summer's day with temperatures over 80°F. Lynn rushed onto the sidewalk, as the street traffic was very heavy. She opened her purse again as she began heading in the direction of the main entrance. She reassured herself that she did indeed have a phone with her.

She retrieved her sunglasses before closing her purse again and placed the dark framed glasses onto her face. She noticed a rather anxious looking man standing outside smoking a cigarette. He happened to be standing right next to the sign proudly stating the hospital had a smoke free campus. It was just one of the many incredible things happening there.

Lynn couldn't help smirking at the irony. When Lynn got closer, he dropped the cigarette, having only smoked half of it, and stamped it out with his foot. He turned to head back inside, but didn't see Lynn there and knocked into her.

"Sorry, my wife is in labor. I…" he began, with his voice trailing off. He stood about 6'1" tall and wore jeans and a green shaggy jacket over a black T-shirt. Lynn glanced back up at the sign.

"Indeed, incredible," she remarked and proceeded inside to the main reception desk.

"Hey, my sister was brought here after a fire at the house she was visiting?" Lynn asked politely.

"Name?" the receptionist asked, with a tone as monotonous and uncaring as anyone could ever imagine.

"Her name is Raven. She is my sister," Lynn lied. Since the lady appeared so emotionless, Lynn believed she could have told her she was the First Lady, but she would still just ask for a name.

"When was she brought here?" the woman responded.

"2 days ago. The fire EMS brought her here," Lynn answered flatly. She knew smiles were contagious, and apparently being an asshole was too.

"3rd floor, section 42B. Was moved from the ICU yesterday. Down the hall, turn right, you will find the elevators. Have a nice day," the receptionist stated with an automated quality to her voice.

"Why don't you just quit if you don't like this job so much?" Lynn asked before walking away. She couldn't help herself.

"Because I like eating, and I have free healthcare from this health network for working here," she replied.

"Kind of a cheap price for your soul," Lynn commented, as she dropped a $20 bill in the tip jar and headed down the hall toward the elevators.

Leaving all thoughts of that woman behind, she once again set her focus on her objective. She found the turn to the right and eventually found the elevators. On the ride up, Lynn's phone started to vibrate. She successfully retrieved it from her purse as the elevator paused to allow more people inside. She read the text message and flipped her phone open to reply.

"I'm here now. I haven't heard anything more about the trip. Talk soon."

Lynn returned the phone to her purse just as the elevator doors opened on the third floor. She exited into a mass of people busying around the floor, including nurses, doctors, and wandering patients. Unsure which way to turn, Lynn quickly hunted for a directional sign. Short term inpatients were to the left, whereas wards 1-48 for long term inpatients were straight ahead.

"Can I help you? You look lost, honey," one of the nurses asked, startling Lynn. She was cute. She had unique red hair with a nice smile and stood about 5'7" tall. She wore light blue kitten themed scrubs and was looking directly at Lynn.

"Oh, what? Oh, yes, thanks. I'm looking for my sister, Raven. She was brought in here two days ago. Section 42B the front lady said?" Lynn responded. She noticed the nurse's name tag read *Megan*.

"Right down here."–Megan pointed down the right hallway–"She still unconscious. She has several burns on her. They found her under some of the rubble. The blast of the fire was focused upward and out, not sideways. She was located in the basement according to the EMS," Megan reported, as they made their way down the hall.

"Did they bring anyone else out?" Lynn questioned.

"Not that I'm aware of; although, they could have gone to other hospitals. You know what she was doing there?" Megan inquired.

"She was visiting. She is on holiday from England for the weekend. She was friends with the boy, Michael. That was his house. I'm friends with Courtney, Michael's sister, and Raven is my sister," Lynn explained, only slightly bending the truth towards the end.

"Well, she still unconscious, as I said. You are welcome to sit with her. I have to warn you; don't be frightened by all the screens and monitors, okay? She's in here." Megan stopped, turned, and pointed into a private room.

Heeding the nurse's warning, Lynn took a deep breath in and opened the door. The curtains were drawn closed, keeping the room dark. She could hear a rhythmic pumping sound coming from the IV monitor, as it pumped steady amounts of saline and medicine into Raven from the 2 bags hanging on the IV stand.

"Is she in pain?" Lynn questioned, with a concerned look on her face. She glanced at the EKG marching and other support machines hooked up to Raven.

"No, we gave her 50cc of morphine 2 hours ago via her IV. If you want anything, just let one us know or push the button. We're right outside the door," Megan said comfortingly, as she left the room and closed the door. Lynn slowly approached the right side of the bed and pulled one of the chairs closer to be able to sit by Raven's side.

"Well, I guess Chris picked well. You must be strong to have survived," Lynn muttered, as she reached out to grab her hand. However, she pulled back after noticing Raven's hands and most of her arms were covered by a sort of sealed wrap to help the burns heal. "If it's any consolation, I didn't want this for you. I'm glad Chris had found someone; I always knew he had to when I left."

Lynn heard Megan's voice returning, followed by the familiar voice of her *friend*, Sgt. Wilkinson. Lynn grabbed her phone to send a quick text.

He's here. You are clear to go in. She hit send just as the door opened.

Wilkinson walked straight up to the bed and placed handcuffs on the only clear area of skin on Raven's unconscious right arm.

"What are you doing?!" Lynn protested.

"She is the only survivor of a multiple homicide. The signal that detonated the explosion came from her phone," he remarked, looking at Lynn sternly.

"Rubbish. She wouldn't blow herself up. What reason would she have? Besides, she isn't going anywhere. If you haven't noticed, she isn't exactly in a condition to flee!"

Megan left in a hurry, as she had been standing by the door watching the confrontation.

"It is still being investigated; however, she is the lead suspect," he explained.

"It makes no sense. Do you have any actual evidence that she did it? She is a tourist. It was the very first time she visited the house. To commit homicide, you need to plan it out. It isn't something you do on the spur of the moment."–Lynn looked down at Raven and back up to Wilkinson–"Besides, she has an alibi. She was with Michael since she arrived in the country and was at a HIM concert and stayed with Michael the entire time."

"Well, sadly, Michael is dead, so there goes her alibi," Wilkinson interrupted.

"Do I have to help you with your investigation? Go check the hotel she is staying at. Go to the concert hall. They have security cameras, I'm sure, and they will have her ticket stubbed. Anyway, you do not have enough for probable cause to place cuffs on an unconscious patient, who is suffering from 3rd degree burns, who is not a flight risk. You are in violation, Wilkinson. You should really brush up on your criminal justice skills," Lynn taunted.

Wilkinson was about to argue when a doctor burst into the room, followed by Megan.

"I don't know what this is about. Regardless, under the New York Health Code Act, you cannot place a burn victim or a unconscious person in cuffs unless you have a court order signed by a judge," the doctor reported. Wilkinson ignored the doctor completely, and kept his eyes focused directly on Lynn.

"Where is she?" Wilkinson demanded.

"Who?" Lynn responded, keeping her eyes trained on him without shifting.

"My partner, Sarah. I last saw her at her apartment. She was going to see you and they found her car abandoned at the scene of the explosion," he elaborated.

"Oh... I see you were at her apartment. I didn't know you two were serious?" Lynn replied with a question of her own. "You sure this is business and not personal?"

"Just answer the question, dammit," Wilkinson pushed.

"I haven't seen *Sarah* since the night of the club when you were getting schooled. Perhaps she went into the house trying to save the people inside and got caught up in the fire?" Lynn offered.

In the next moment, hospital security arrived. They were definitely not accustomed to escorting police out of the hospital, as they normally escorted them in.

"Remove the handcuffs, officer, and then I'll be requiring your badge ID," the doctor ordered.

He stared Wilkinson down, as the cuffs were removed. Wilkinson glanced towards Lynn one more time, while the security placed a hand under his right arm to lead him out of the room. The doctor followed them, leaving Megan behind.

"I'm sorry you had to go through that. You okay?" Megan asked gently.

"Yeah, I'm fine. It's no problem. Thanks though," Lynn replied, as she sat back down at Raven's bedside. She snatched up her phone to send another text.

He's gone. He's in love with you. She finished typing and hit send.

Megan made sure everything was back to normal. Then she turned and left, softly closing the door behind her.

Lynn focused her attention back to Raven, who continued to lie there, completely unaware of the events that just took place.

"Well, Raven, I said I would explain and tell you what happened. I guess now is as good a time as any."

4 CHAPTER FOUR

A very gusty morning, the daylight was just starting to emerge from the horizon. It would still be a few hours before the sun began to show itself. Chris stepped up to the doors of NWI the following morning, as the bus he arrived on started to depart. Aside from himself, only a couple of other people got off the bus, though he ignored them and kept to himself.

"Too bloody early," Chris mumbled under his breath. He entered the airport looking for the BHS Outlet, hoping he could at least get something to eat or drink to help him feel more awake.

However, his hopes quickly drifted away when he saw the shutters covering the BHS outlet. Sighing, he settled on heading to the Boots Outlet. He bought some Walker's Salt 'n Vinegar Squares, his favorite kind of potato chips. One of the books on the shelf caught his eye, *A Throne for Sisters* by Morgan Rice. He picked up the book to read the back cover.

Chris usually wasn't much for reading books; he typically found it difficult to get drawn into the stories or role. He had trouble picturing the characters and such in his mind. He could count on one hand the number of books he had ever read. He remembered reading *The Long, The Short, and the Tall* in high school. He had enjoyed it because it was set during World War II, which was a time period that had always interested Chris.

The very first book he recalled reading just for fun was *Ghostbusters II*. He was drawn in much easier than with other books. He had already seen the movie as well, which helped him be able to picture the characters more easily too.

Next, it was *Sharpe's Eagle* and *Sharpe's Rifles* from the *Richard Sharpe* series, written by Bernard Cornwell. Chris had been a longtime fan of the TV series and seeing Sean Bean playing the role of Sharpe, the down trodden soldier who rose through the ranks to become an officer. He visualized Sean Bean for Sharpe as he read, which made it fairly easy for him to be drawn into the books. He found there were several details in the books that had been left out in the TV series, so it was like discovering the series for the first time all over again.

With technology constantly advancing, Chris always found a way to avoid holding an actual book. He found it easy to read on his cellphone or computer. E-readers were also becoming more and more prevalent, though it was still kind of a new experience to him.

Chris preferred to enjoy books in audio form. He kind of inherited the habit from his mother; she would love to listen to audiobooks in the car. Every so often, she would go to the town library to rent books to read. She would also pick out audiobooks on cassette tapes to listen to in the car. She volunteered to drive the elderly and other people who were unable to drive to take them to doctors' appointments, to stores, or to other places. She made a lot of friends, who were very grateful for the rides. While driving between destinations and while waiting for her riders at various places, Chris' mother took advantage of all her time in the car to listen to books on tape.

He remembered that every time she picked him up from school, some sort of story would always be playing, like the Harry Potter books. He eventually started renting and listening to his own audiobooks. He even aspired to record his own audiobooks one day.

Placing the book back on the shelf, he added a note on his phone with the name of the book for him to search for it online later. It was still a bit early; the plane wasn't due to arrive until 7:50pm. The bus he came on was the only one expected to arrive at the airport ahead of time. The other would have been 44 minutes late.

Chris hadn't received any recent messages from Courtney except to say she was on the way, but that was 9 hours ago. He hadn't heard anything from Raven either, though he hoped she read his letter.

He needed to try to give her an explanation. Everything he has done was all for her. He knew it was word play, but technically, he wasn't lying and he didn't break his promise to Raven. He had promised to not help her. She did not explicitly say she didn't want help, and also did not make Chris specifically promise to not ask for help from someone else.

He knew something was clearly wrong. Raven had put herself in harm's way to protect her family. Now, she needed protecting. He hoped she would understand.

His love for her was true. He had grown to care for her very much. He promised her he loved her so much he would sacrifice everything to keep her safe and happy, even if that meant sacrificing her loving him. He knew Lynn's reputation. He wasn't a fool. He knew Raven may hate him for tricking her, but he needed her out the way, so they could deal with her father.

You know in your heart what is right and what is wrong. It is wrong to stand back and do nothing while you know someone you love is being hurt, even if they made you promise to do nothing.

Chris reasoned that he would prove just how much he cared for her by showing he cared more for her happiness and welfare than his own.

However, she was now nine thousand miles away from him, where anything could happen to her. He knew Lynn's style, but he hoped Lynn would be coming there.

Chris was about to find out as he heard an announcement come over the intercom. Lynn's plane was due to land in 5 minutes. He got up and walked across to the observation window, near where the arriving passengers would enter the terminal.

As the plane slowly came into view over the horizon, he sent the message to Courtney as instructed. *"Plane in sight."*

Inside the plane, Courtney felt the g-force as the plane began its descent toward the runway. Thankfully, the flight felt much shorter than it actually was. She had been able to sleep through most of it, as they were following the Earth's rotation by flying to England.

She gripped the armrests and watched through the window. She saw the buildings on the ground suddenly start to grow larger and larger. From the air above, she noticed the main contrast between England and America were their sports fields. In America, it seemed like there were baseball fields on every other block. However, in England, soccer fields scattered the land.

Courtney didn't really know what to expect, as Lynn didn't really prepare her all that much. She had only provided a single picture of Chris, so she would be able to recognize him.

The plane hit the ground at full speed, jolting everyone inside, before immediately starting to slow its speed.

Chris could feel the anxiety rising within him, as he watched the plane zoom past the window. As it approached the end of the runway, the plane slowed to crawl before turning to taxi toward the terminal.

After the plane came to a complete stop, the door opened, and fresh air swept in throughout the cabin. It was very refreshing, like waking from a long nap. Courtney stood up, quickly retrieved her carry-on, and proceeded toward the exit.

Courtney hesitated as she approached the door, drawing out the moment before nervously crossing the threshold.

"Welcome back, Lynn," Chris announced, with a smile beaming across his face. "How was the flight?"

"Restful. It is a shame I cannot just hop onto a plane the next time I have insomnia. Where is the car rental store, please? I have a reservation," Courtney remarked, smiling.

"Oh, right over here, I'll show you. Here, let me get that, so you can have your hands free."–he noticed her eyes as he leaned in to grab her luggage– "It's right over here," Chris said, pointing.

"Thanks. How come you haven't got your license?" Courtney questioned.

"I've come close to passing; it's just hard. It'd be easy for me if we drove on the right. My main hand is left, so driving manual kind of gets uncoordinated," Chris explained.

"Oh well, I'm sure you will get it. Should just switch to automatic," Courtney suggested. She retrieved her rental car information from her purse as she approached the counter. Chris stepped back.

A man, only 5'6" tall, stepped up to the desk. He was smartly dressed in a cashmere sweater, grey dress shirt, black tie, and black slacks. His name tag read *David*.

"Hello! Reservation, driver's license, and proof of insurance, please," the man requested.

Chris had stepped back to give her privacy. It took about 8 minutes to get all the paper work done before the keys were handed over to Courtney.

She turned, to see Chris looking like a puppy with his head sort of tilted to the side.

"Ready?" she asked with a smile.

"Sure. Let's go," Chris said slowly, as a smile crept across his face. "It's nice to meet you, Courtney."

She didn't say a word, but just kept walking. Chris followed behind her, as they headed out of the terminal toward the rental car parking lot.

"What gave me away?" Courtney inquired, as they continued walking.

"Your eyes. You have softer eyes; you're gentler too," Chris responded. "Don't feel bad. I've known her for a long time."

"Poor puppy," Courtney sighed.

"Huh?" Chris replied, not fully hearing her.

"Oh, nothing. Lynn is wanting me to use her name while I'm here. She said it would protect me. So, no one must know; to everyone else, I'm Lynn," Courtney explained.

They paused at the edge of the lot. She pressed the key fob and waited to see which car's lights flashed. Then they headed off in its direction.

"I understand the strategy behind what she is doing. There is only one problem," Chris stated.

"… and what is that?" Courtney questioned.

"Have I been talking to you the entire time, or is Lynn on your name?" he asked, as he passed his phone to Courtney, so she could see the messages he had been sending and receiving from her account.

Courtney started walking toward the left side of the car, but stopped and turned back to head to the right side of the car, while Chris placed her luggage in the boot of the car. He hid a small laugh as he noticed her mistake.

He closed the boot, then hurried to get in the passenger side on the left. He saw she was reading through the messages on his phone.

"I didn't send any of these to you. I only knew she was on my account before we left when we swapped accounts," Courtney stated, handing Chris's phone back to him. "So, what is the problem?"

"Well, it won't be a problem for me to keep your secret; however, you posted under Lynn's name that you are here in England. Someone is going to be very hurt or upset with her when they find out you are not Lynn. And, if we go out of our way to completely avoid them, they will, again, be upset. Did she give you a way to contact her?" Chris questioned.

"No, she said she would call me. I have to wait until then." Courtney started the car and pulled out to head to her hotel.

"Who are you talking about?" Courtney asked.

Chris paused for a moment before answering.

"Her mom."

4.2 CHAPTER FOUR POINT TWO

The door to Raven's hospital room opened slowly, interrupting Lynn. The nurse stepped aside to allow the new visitor to enter.

After entering, the young person watched the nurse close the door again. She waited until the door was fully shut before removing her coat and hanging it on the back of one of the chairs.

"Well, I see you are, once again, two steps ahead of us. Your plan worked; although, I wish it didn't involve the store. A little more warning next time… maybe, please?" Lola expressed towards Lynn.

Lola was completely disheveled. She appeared as though she had slept in her clothes. Her very formal grey clothing, to be exact, which included a knee length skirt, black stockings, grey suit jacket, and black tie.

"I don't have the defense codes for Zion, Agent Lola," Lynn joked, mocking Lola as she removed her black sunglasses. Lola just stared back at Lynn, not returning the smile.

"Okay… not the time for jokes, Agent."–Lynn stood up and laughed at her own joke–"You want to tell me what happened? After, I mean. I guess if you are here, they haven't arrested you."–Lynn stepped close to Lola–"Not that they could. The most they could pin on you was negligence, and you have liability insurance to cover things like this, right?"

"If it could be proved an accident, not intentional or homicide, which they are currently taking it as, so the insurance isn't paying out until that is complete. Not that it would matter. This will ruin the reputation of the store.

Would you want to get your hair done where someone got electrocuted?" Lola stated, placing her hands on her hips.

"Sure, they would. There're going to be those curious that will tweet they survived Credo's," Lynn commented, with a smile. "If you brand and promote this right, it could help to make Credo's bigger and better."–Lynn paused for a moment, looking at Lola–"It's good to see you again…" Lynn remarked, suddenly changing the pace of the conversation. She hugged Lola.

"You too, Miss Spoonman," Lola replied softly, finally taking part in the Matrix joke. "So, who is this?" Lola inquired, pointing at Raven.

"The girlfriend of the lost puppy," Lynn responded simply.

"You don't mince words, do you? You said you would punish Mrs. Howard and look how she ended up. So, what happened with Courtney?" Lola questioned.

"I was explaining just that to Raven here. I promised I would tell her what happened to her father; however, things got in the way," Lynn reported, with a sad expression on her face. Lola was taken aback, having never before seen Lynn express remorse.

"You actually regret what happened to her?" Lola asked, sounding surprised.

"I promised Chris I would look after her while she was here. I didn't get to spend much time with her except on the ride to her hotel. From what I did and talking to her, I liked."–Lynn sighed–"However, the plan didn't go perfectly. I underestimated Raven."

"So, you not exactly sorry. More like you are sorry she survived?" Lola suggested.

"I wouldn't put it like that exactly. I'm more surprised I wanted to see how well Chris picked. I mean to say, I wanted to see if her strength was out of ignorance or is it because she actually knows. However, it appears she is a survivor."–Lynn walked back to Raven's side–"I think she may be one of us."

"Perhaps you should put a leash on that puppy of yours. He seems to have a talent of finding strong bitches like us." Lola moved to put an arm around Lynn's shoulder.

"It is okay to feel jealousy if you still like him," Lola commented. Lynn's head snapped up instantly at Lola's words.

"You used his name. You are also being very protective over someone you claim not to like," Lola explained, answering Lynn's quizzical look. "Perhaps you liked him liking you, and that he still liked you even after you moved. Then suddenly that went away, and now our friend Raven is here."

"How long are you planning on staying here?" Lola inquired.

"Until she wakes up, if I let her wake up," Lynn mused. "However, I want her to see me here when or if she does. She could be even better than Courtney," Lynn remarked, silently considering how she could twist and manipulate their friendship to her advantage. Lynn turned her back, signaling the conversation was over.

Lola started to head toward the door to make her way out of the room.

"Let me know how much the fine is," Lynn commented, just as Lola reached the door. "I have the means to pay it off."

Lola froze, toying with the idea of asking Lynn how she had the means. However, she decided better of it, thinking some things are best left unknown. Lola continued walking and left the room.

~

Over on West 57th in New York City, Sarah crept towards her apartment door. She received the text that Blue was out, just as she found the door had been left ajar. Sarah immediately felt annoyed because he apparently left her apartment door unlocked and open. She listened for anyone who could be inside.

Sarah reached into her cleavage and pulled out her *Lady* as she approached the door. It had been two days since the incident, but Sarah knew they wouldn't need to search the apartment. Her partner had been the last to leave, following their night of fun.

She looked up and saw a barely visible strand of hair balanced on top of the door, stretching to the inside of the frame, taped on either end.

"Not bad at all, Blue," Sarah muttered under her breath. She slipped through the door sideways, being extremely careful not to dislodge the strand of hair.

She took a deep breath in to flatten her chest as much as possible to allow her to squeeze through the opening.

Sarah placed Lady back in her holster as she marched into the bedroom. To her surprise, she noticed the bed had been made.

"OMG, he got me flowers after sex!" Sarah muttered to herself. Making her feel even more guilty, she noticed the bouquet of roses on the bedside table. A single rose laid on the bed with a note. She really wanted to read it, but she fought the urge, as she was trying to make it appear that no one was there.

She walked to the closet to open it. *"He's a man; they only notice stuff that's right under their nose,"* she thought. Sarah suddenly turned on the spot and went straight to the card lying on the bed. It read:

I don't know if you'll ever read this, I don't know what happened. Thank you for giving me an education I will never forget. I hope to be able to put into practice what you taught me. The last time I saw you was when you were going off to find her and then you vanished. Your car was deserted and there has been no sign of you. Everyone is trying to tell me you died inside the house fire. I don't believe it. It's the club all over again. I miss you already. I will never believe you are gone until I see your body. The captain is oddly silent about you. He has refused to classify you as dead, but instead, absent without leave. Whatever is going on, just please trust me and reach out to me.

Signed, Blue
P.S. I think I deserve a promotion in your ranking system.
P.P.S. Please come back to me. You can call me whatever you want, just please don't be dead.

As Sarah finished reading the note, she felt her left eye starting to betray her. She quickly regained her composure and placed the note back where she found it. She opened the closet and retrieved a bag from deep inside. Hurriedly, she gathered a selection of clothing that she knew Blue wouldn't notice was missing.

She then dropped to her knees and pulled a wooden military style foot-locker size box out from under the bed. She opened it to reveal a smaller solid 9"x5" oak box, with a leather interior held in place with copper lining the corners and framing each side. A neodymium magnet laid inside the box. She had swiped during her time in the Police Academy. At the time, Sarah had a gut feeling that it would be useful to her in the future, she just never thought it would be for a reason like this.

She retrieved the phone that previously belonged to Courtney's dad, the one

Lynn had tricked Sarah into using. Sarah had used the "call me" feature to respond to a text; however, Lynn was using the remote feature via iCloud accounts to send the text from a phone she had set up in Credo's. This phone was intended to kill Mrs. Howard, aka Mrs. Hemlock, a con artist.

Sarah held in her hand evidence of Lynn committing a class E felony under the New York Penal Law, section 155.30(6). Sarah knew the law well enough, but so did Lynn. This phone was used to transfer money into Lynn's account and received texts blackmailing her victim, and yet, it was also the phone that would send Sarah away for a very long time.

Lynn had made sure there was record of her tracing the phone. The original trace she did was to find out where Courtney's dad was, but she had kept going. She knew Sarah had the phone, so there would be enough doubt for a jury to not totally believe that Lynn was blackmailing the victim and knowingly tricking Sarah; therefore, not a felony or extortion, but rather a felony for the New York Statute Penal Law, section 125.27, better known as Murder 1, which carries a sentence of death. This is why Sarah found herself in her current predicament. Lynn had safely backed up all the data in an encrypted lock-up somewhere on the dark web as insurance.

The only thing Sarah could think of to protect herself, and ultimately Lynn too, was to completely wipe the phone. She stared at the phone, briefly weighing up her options. Sarah knew she had exactly what her former partner needed to send his perp to jail for a long time, and then… and then he would go home, she suspected.

This last thought inspired her to carry on. She dropped the phone into the box and closed the lid. She then added the entire box into the bag with her clothes. Back in the foot locker, Sarah retrieved all the ammunition she had for her *Lady*. She also retrieved a small aluminum case with a combination lock, more boxes of ammunition, and all the holsters she had, including the standard issued shoulder holster. Sarah remembered the look on her instructor's face when they realized it wasn't going to fit on her well-developed chest. For the duration of the training, they made her wear a belt holster; however, at graduation, one of the female instructors had gotten her the bra holster.

Sarah was jolted from her moment of nostalgia as the phone began to vibrate. A text from Lynn appeared on the screen.

"Poor Blue," she remarked, as she read the text. She couldn't stand the guilt of hurting him.

She stood up and pushed the box back under the bed with her foot. She reached to grab the card again and flipped it over. She wrote something on the back and placed it back under the rose. She walked around the bed to smell the bouquet of flowers. She pulled one out from the bouquet, broke off the stem, and slid it through one of the buttonholes on her shirt.

She grabbed her bag and began to make her way out of the apartment. She also snagged a couple bottles of wine. Sarah didn't want to leave those here for whoever visited next, and she knew she would want a drink after this was over.

"Ah, you sneaky bastard!" Sarah exclaimed, as she reached the front door. She examined the hair on top of the door. She could tell it wasn't hers; it was a different color, most likely Chenelle's, so Sarah couldn't simply replace it with one of her own.

She moved a dining chair closer to the door and climbed on top of it. She slowly peeled the tape off the door, being careful to prevent removing any paint with it, and delicately lifted the single strand of hair away from the door. She then opened the door wider, put the chair back in its place, and dumped her bag in the hallway. She glanced back as she stepped out of the apartment and pulled the door back to its original position. Finally, she reattached the tape with the hair to the top of the door and she was gone.

Later that night, a ragged looking Wilkinson walked up to the hallway toward Sarah's apartment, hoping by some miracle she was home. When he reached the door, he felt let down as he saw the hair was still there. However, he knelt down, and with his hand, he checked behind the door to see if the dime was still propped up against the door.

"It's flat!" Wilkinson announced. He jumped up instantly, pushing the door open. He stormed in calling, "Sarah! Sarah! You here?!"

He searched through the apartment, but came to the realization that she wasn't there after all. The dime must have just fallen over on its own. He walked into the bedroom to find the room was exactly the way he left it.

He checked the bathroom, but nope, she was not there either. Sighing as he stepped back into the bedroom, he walked over to the bed and sat down, feeling extremely disappointed. The movement of the bed as he sat down dislodged the rose and card he had left for Sarah. He picked up the rose and held it in his hands, smelling it briefly.

"I miss you, partner," he said, with another heavy sigh.

Wilkinson placed the flower back on the bed, and then noticed the card. He picked up the card and reread his own words. Nope, they hadn't changed, but when he flipped the card over, he received the biggest surprise. His disappointed frown immediately turned into the biggest smile as he read the note Sarah had written.

You're right, I'm promoting you to Red.

Christopher Blythe Bartram

6 CHAPTER SIX

"I hate being interrupted anyway. Where was I?" Lynn stated, as she turned back to Raven's side.

Chris escorted Courtney up to her hotel room with her bags in tow. Chris had attempted to contact Lynn on Courtney's Facebook account except the chat feature was turned off, or it had been blocked. As a result, they were going to be forced to carry on as is for now, and worry about the little oversight for Lynn to sort out. Courtney slid the key card in the slot and opened the door.

"I should stay with you. Lynn told me I should stay by your side while you are here," Chris explained.

"Oh okay, I was just going to go to sleep, nothing exciting," Courtney stated. Chris put a hand out to stop her from entering the room. He stepped in front of her and entered briefly to set her bags down. Then he turned around, stepped back out of the room, and swept her off her feet, into his arms.

"If something is worth doing, it's worth doing right!" Chris smiled at Courtney. She was completely surprised with a big smile across her face.

"This only applies if you're just married, silly," Courtney laughed, as Chris carried her into the room and pushed the door closed with his foot.

"Oh, should I put you back, so you can walk in?" Chris teased.

"No, no, this is fine," Courtney quickly responded, unsure if Chris was being serious or not.

"Besides, the floor could be lava! You just never know!" Chris joked, as a smile spread across his face.

The hotel room contained two double beds with a desk by the window. A TV sat on the dresser, facing the beds.

"Ah, the English 101 essential item: tea! Oh, they have some Nescafé coffee here," Courtney commented, browsing the selection laid out on the dresser.

"I wouldn't touch the coffee," Chris warned. "Although I know America is a nation of coffee drinkers, England is not. You would only want to drink that stuff if you like drinking piss water. However, if you really want coffee,"–Chris walked over to Courtney, pulling a box from his pants pocket–"I hear you guys run on this!" he exclaimed proudly, as he held up a small box of Dunkin' Donuts coffee.

"OMG. You wouldn't happen to have a chocolate donut in there too, do you?" Courtney laughed. "I guess not. I assume you just have the normal cream-filled éclair?"–Courtney winked–"Thanks for the coffee though; I'm going to save it. I'm here, so I might as well try some of the tea."

"Okay, I'll be mother. You go freshen up or something," Chris stated, as he walked up to start preparing the tea.

"Be mother?" Courtney questioned, sounding puzzled.

"Oh, it means the person who pours. It is really bad luck if more than one person pours or makes the tea, so the first person to pour or make the tea is called 'mother'. There is a whole process and set of rules to make a proper English cuppa," Chris explained.

"Show me," Courtney requested.

"Okay. Is this the first time you ever had hot tea?" Chris inquired. Courtney nodded in response. "Okay then, I'll put milk and a lil bit of sugar in. I won't put too much in and just let you decide after."

He carried the hotel's standard-issue kettle into the bathroom and filled it with water from the tap. Upon returning to the main room, he plugged the kettle in to heat the water.

He searched through the small cups and found the milks. He picked up four initially, but after looking back at Courtney, he selected two more milks.

He poured four milks into one cup for Courtney, and two into the other cup for himself. He rummaged through all the sample bags of tea and picked out the best ones, labeled PG Tips. He dropped two tea bags into the kettle.

"One bag for each person or one bag for the number of cups you want," Chris noted.

"Where'd you learn this?" Courtney wondered aloud.

"My mum, and she learned it from her mum," Chris reported.

"I guess that is where the term came from then, as it is often your mothers that pour the tea?" Courtney suggested, as they waited for the water to boil.

"It would make sense. The tradition was observed a lot, if not started, in WWI. Those in the Air Force were very superstitious, not wanting to do anything that would curse them or give them bad luck before they went up on a flight. So, in the mess when they had tea, they made sure of who was 'mother,' so they wouldn't give themselves bad luck," Chris explained. "There is a story on Wikipedia of one pilot who poured his own second cup of tea. He was shot down the next day, so they took it seriously."

As the water began to boil, he picked up the kettle and poured it into the hotel-provided teapot.

"What is the point of the pot?" Courtney questioned.

"It filters the tea to make sure none of the tea leaves get into your drink. You are supposed to let the tea stand for a moment before pouring; however, I give the pot a little shake and that does the job," Chris responded, as he finally poured the tea.

"You make a good mother," Courtney stated proudly. She smiled as she picked up the teacup. Chris dropped two sugar cubes into her tea and left the bowl near her in case she wanted more.

He sat down on the end of the bed directly opposite the TV and turned it on with the remote. He patted the bed next to him, indicating for Courtney to sit down, and she did.

"*House* should be on," Chris announced.

"Oh, I love *House*," Courtney replied excitedly.

"Liar," Chris challenged.

"No, I really do love *House*," Courtney protested.

"Everybody lies," the narrator's voice projected from the TV. Chris pointed and smiled at his well-timed joke.

They both settled into enjoying the show while drinking their tea. Chris made a sideward glance toward Courtney, making sure her attention was on the show. As his eyes returned to the TV, he slid his right hand onto her left leg and slowly started to rub the inside of her thigh. His hand gradually slid up her leg, as if it had a mind of its own.

Chris continued rubbing with his third and fourth fingers, and used his thumb and index finger to slowly undo the button on Courtney's pants. He slipped his hand down onto the outside of her panties. She started to breathe heavier, but she maintained her focus on the TV, as she was kind of enjoying the show. Chris kept rubbing more heavily but she continued to watch the show ignoring what Chris was doing as she was kind of enjoying it. He kept rubbing until he felt her starting to get wet. He pulled her panties to the side in order to slip his second and third fingers inside her vagina, while he kept rubbing outside with his other fingers. Courtney let out a loud moan.

"Having fun?" Chris suggested, as he turned to her with a smile across his face.

"Uh huh," Courtney replied, seemingly unable to speak in full words. She looked down. "Hey! When did you get into my pants?!" she exclaimed. Chris stood up instantly.

"I want you. Now." He pulled her up from the bed by her hand and swept her off her feet again. He seductively threw her onto the other bed. As she landed on the soft bed, she turned to find Chris watching her with a very hungry stare in his eyes. He found her impossible to resist. Courtney was slightly frightened by the look in his eyes. He undid the button on his pants and let them drop to the floor as he walked up to her. She turned onto her knees in a playful attempt to get away. He pulled her back, flipped her over, and pulled off her pants. He then used his knee to climb onto the bed and paused for a moment.

"You okay with this?" Chris questioned, looking directly at her. He wanted her consent to make sure it was okay for him to proceed. She nodded, but he waited for a verbal response. Upon getting the response he desired, he flipped

Courtney back over onto her knees, grabbed the back of her hair and slid his full length inside her. Chris pulled on Courtney's hair to give mixed sensations of pain and pleasure.

With his free hand, Chris reached around Courtney's torso to grab hold of her breast through her shirt. He could feel the sensation of being inside her grow with each passing moment. He turned Courtney onto her back again as he continued to pleasure her. Chris felt her muscles tightening around his length. He leaned forward and slid his hand up her shirt. Chris had been fairly silent, not wanting to waste energy by moaning, as he concentrated on pleasuring Courtney. He bent forward more, so as to thrust deeper inside Courtney, hitting her cervix. Courtney bit Chris's shoulder seductively. He started to growl and thrusted harder. Chris began to act more animalistic, as he had totally zoned out, which took Courtney by surprise. However, she was *really* enjoying their tryst. Courtney could feel vibrations up into her chest as Chris began thrusting even harder.

Chris's phone laid forgotten on the desk. Neither of them noticed the red light turn on when Lynn attempted to respond to Chris's attempts to chat with her. When she didn't get a response, she decided to remotely turn on the phone's camera. It turned out she was just in time to clearly understand what was preventing Chris from responding, as she heard Chris begin to roar.

"Oh, fuck yeah, Lynn. I knew you love cock," Chris roared, loud enough that Lynn heard him through the phone's mic.

Courtney rested her hand on Chris's chest and pressed up, only to feel him fire inside of her. The exhilarating sensation completely distracted her, as she enveloped Chris into her arms. The continued firing made Courtney combust and climax with him still inside her. Chris laid his face down on the bed next to Courtney's head. She could tell he was trying to catch his breath as if he had just ran a marathon.

"How many times was that?" Courtney questioned.

"I lost count after four," he replied breathlessly.

"So much for the myth that men can only go once," she stated, as a smile spread across her face.

"All it takes is stamina, concentration, and the will to keep going and push through the wall. Each one feels better than the last," Chris explained, as he rolled over onto his back.

"I'm sorry. I don't know what came over me. I just had to have you there and then. I saw you and it was like water over filling and bursting its dam," Chris remarked, still breathing heavily.

"You remember calling me Lynn?" Courtney asked, which resulted in a sharp look back from Chris.

"I only remember leaning forward, then you bit me. Next thing I remember was feeling you hugging onto me, both with your arms and with your lady parts," Chris admitted.

"So, you don't remember roaring then?" she continued.

"Roaring?" He was starting to feel a bit embarrassed now.

"Yeah, it was kind of wild and hot," Courtney giggled. "You were all silent, then when I bit you, you totally changed. I guess you were seeing pink." Courtney propped herself up on her arm.

"Seeing pink?" Chris asked, sounding puzzled.

"Yes, I guess you could say it is an American term. Just like when someone gets into a rage, or where someone is not aware of their actions, and instincts take over, it is called seeing red. Well, not to sound too much like the Merovingian, but everything has an opposite and equal reaction. If there is blind rage built up from hate and anger, then there is also blind passion, the ultimate feeling of love–seeing 'pink'," Courtney explained.

She playfully began to push Chris off the bed with her feet.

"I'm tired and I want to rest now. Your attempts to steal the bed next to the window will not be successful. Although, I applaud your attempt," Courtney stated with a wink.

Chris got up and walked across the room to the other bed.

"How come you never told Lynn how much you loved her?" Courtney questioned.

"What good would it have done? I would have only gotten in the way. I'm one of many that liked her," he replied, as he started to turn down the bed covers.

"But?" Courtney attempted to interject.

"It would do no good. I know I loved her, but I also knew I was nothing to her, one of many boys who did her bidding in hope of winning her favor. Except events overtook things, like I keep saying to myself, I know Lynn's reputation… but I still asked her for her help with Raven because I love Raven just as much, and goodness knows how this will affect you, as you appear to be in the middle of it. You were made to look a lot like Lynn, and yet, I know you are not Lynn. You came here to help me with Raven and I really do appreciate it. I do, really."–Chris turned suddenly and stepped up to the side of Courtney's bed–"I am really sorry if I hurt you or offended you by any of this. You are really kind for helping me out."

Courtney sat up and grasped his hands in hers.

"It is fine. It was just sex, meaningless sex. We fucked. It isn't like we've known each other for ages or dating. Sure, it was a little disconcerting when you used another woman's name while with me. It's not exactly flattering. Yet, now I know you were in that state, it makes sense. You withheld all that emotion and the feelings you have for Lynn, and with me looking like her, it was enough to push you over the edge. Next time you see her or speak to her, you are going to tell her how you feel, or I will. It isn't a crime to love two women, but you do both of them a disservice when you lie to yourself and them.

"Lynn deserves to know how you feel; you don't have the right to be judge and jury. Maybe you are right and Lynn doesn't like you, but you are not going to know if you don't give her the opportunity to answer you. Even if you love Raven and want to be with her, you still need to know the truth about Lynn because you will always be wondering *what if?*"–Courtney laid back down–"Now get some rest. We only got a couple of hours, then we have to plan and organize."

Chris did as instructed and finally climbed into his own bed.

"Oh, Chris?" Courtney mused.

"Hmm?" he responded.

"You felt really good inside… Night!" she said sharply, cutting off any chance of a reply.

The small red light on the phone slowly went black again.

7 CHAPTER SEVEN

The door to the hospital room opened once again, interrupting Lynn in the middle of her retelling recent events.

This time though, she didn't care in the least, as she saw Ann walking in with a small duffle bag.

"OMG, what you doing here?" Lynn jumped up to give Ann a big welcome hug.

"Keep moving," Lola spoke up from behind, as Ann and Lynn quickly moved out of the way. Lola was carrying two Louis Vuitton shopping bags in her hand with a backpack hung over her shoulder.

"Ann, that table will do. Move it to the end of the bed," Lola instructed, as she pointed to table in the corner of the room.

Ann moved all the standard-issue flowers and reading materials on flu vaccines and proper hand washing procedures to the side table.

"What's going on?" Lynn inquired.

"Okay, all you guys should be good," Megan remarked, as she entered the room and closed the door behind her.

"I'm disappointed in you, Lynn. It's Wednesday night. Since you are clearly not leaving here anytime soon, we came to you," Ann reprimanded Lynn. Ann opened the two shopping bags, and pulled out a 24-pack of Yuengling from one and a 24-pack of Magic Hat #9 from the other.

Lola opened the duffle bag and pulled out a rollout hot pink poker tabletop. Before she could roll it out on the table, Megan held out a hand to stop her, and quickly spread a spare clean bed sheet over the table under the poker tabletop.

"The table would stick to your poker top, ruining it," Megan explained.

Lynn had completely forgotten about their weekly "girls-acting-like-guys" night.

"Entry fees, ladies," Lola announced, as she paused and stared at Megan. "Your bra, please."

Megan quickly glanced at Lynn and Ann, who were already removing their own bras and hanging them onto the corner of their chairs.

"It's okay, Megan. It just ensures you are a woman," Lynn explained.

"Don't you think, in these times, that removing panties would be more concrete, considering people are arguing over which bathrooms to use?" Megan pointed out, as she followed suit and slipped off her bra.

"She's smart, that one," Ann remarked, as she was already getting into her party mood. She offered a drink to Megan, who accepted now that she was off duty.

Lynn reached over to grab one of the cans of beer and placed it on the side table next to Raven.

"Okay, as normal, bras get you your initial chips, $600. Louboutins - $100, Essies are $50, Sally Hansons - $10, Sinful Colors - $1. I have a real prize for you ladies, besides the normal $600 in beauty products and all the polishes. Tonight, I have a special prize, 2 Bottles of Azature Black Diamond nail polish–market value of $250,000," Lola announced to the group.

"OMG, you kidding?! That nail polish is worth more than my car!" Megan exclaimed.

"You still want to play?" Lola responded, as a smirk slowly spread across her face.

"Yooo, yeah!" Megan replied with an excited tone. She sat up in her seat as Lola started to deal.

"You imagine leaving the top off of them bottles, letting them dry up?" Ann laughed.

"Oh, that isn't a problem. You just add a little bit of water and they will be good as new!" Megan chimed.

"Leave the tops off of yours too much, do you?" Lynn retorted with a chuckle.

"Yep, learned the hard way, then found out I could have saved a lot of money just by adding water," Megan giggled.

"I will never get used to men wearing makeup," Lynn stated. "Well, no, I can to an extent. Just I will never understand why they want lime green nails," she finished, shuddering.

"I don't know. It's a shame blush doesn't work on some of their beards," Ann stated, followed by a hiccup, as she was really starting to get into her drinking.

"I think you find a shaver will work well with that problem, Ann," Lola joked, as she pulled a deck out of the card shuffler. She received a couple of laughs from the women in response.

"You have to be careful with that though. You have him shave and then you end up looking like his big sister with how young they look clean shaved. I like my man with a beard," Megan commented.

"Don't you hate it though when it scratches your face?" Lynn questioned.

Lola pushed the dealer button to her left in front of Megan. She then proceeded to discard two cards and deal the next round of cards, starting with Lynn, as she was sitting to the left of Megan.

"It only scratches you at first when they just shave. As it grows in, it isn't so bad. Just never let them go down on you when they just shave; their stubble will scratch you up then," Megan explained.

"Learned that the hard way, did you?" Ann asked, laughing. She lifted her cards to inspect them and instantly discarded them back to Lola.

Lola called, pushing an Essie bottle into the center of the table.

"Sadly, yeah, I had one boyfriend who loved oral, but I flat out refused to let him go down on me when he just shaved. It's like rubbing your vag with sandpaper. Call," Megan added. She pushed a Sally Hanson toward the pot, as she was the small blind needing to match the big blind of 100.

"Well, I can't say I know what that is like cause I've never rubbed my vag with sandpaper. Check," Lynn giggled, as she tapped the table.

Lola proceeded to deal the flop. KH, 5D, 2D.

"Still, back to my original point, if it turns out he wears more make-up than me, I don't think he would be my boyfriend for very long. Bet 50," Lynn remarked, starting the bet off as she placed an Essie into the center.

"If he's wearing more make-up than you, he probably shouldn't be dating you anyway," Ann chimed into the conversation.

As Lola lifted up her cards, she noticed how Lynn was attempting to distract everyone with her conversation. However, she wouldn't fall for the trick. She was only holding deuce, three with only the bottom pair, so she folded.

"Your turn, Megan," Lola declared. Megan didn't really respond, but kept her eyes on Lynn's hand playing with her stack of nail polishes.

Lynn continued carrying on her conversation; however, Megan remained silent while mentally considering her options. *You hit on something on the flop— possible K, J or 7, 5.* She peeled up the corners of her two cards. A, A—the bullet.

"Here's your 50, and re-raise you 50."

"Call!" Lynn proclaimed with the snap call.

Lola knocked once on the table and flipped over the turn card. KH, 5D, 2D, 10S.

"Check," Lynn stated without hesitation.

The conversation died out as the game started to get serious between the Lynn and Megan.

So, the turn didn't help her, Megan thought. *Or she's disguising a good hand, but nothing on the community could beat my pair, unless Lynn has two pair.*

"50," Meghan remarked, as she pushed another Essie into the pot.

Lynn instantly called again.

Lola dealt the river. KH, 5D, 2D, 10S, KS.

"200," Lynn bet. Megan sighed heavily, as she mucked her hand.

"I'll show you my hand, if you show me yours," Megan suggested. Lynn flipped her cards, displaying KD and QH.

"Nice hand. I had the bullet," Megan complimented, as Lola scooped up the cards while Lynn cleaned up the polishes.

"I thought you would pay me off at the end with how you kept betting before. Good lay down," Lynn replied with a smile.

~

Over at Farrell's watering hole, a rather miserable looking Wilkinson was sitting at the bar atop one of the bar stools. It was—what?—just 3 or 4 days ago, he was here with his partner. Wilkinson was reminiscing, as he gazed around the bar. He noticed a patch now covered the bullet hole Sarah had made.

The drunk captain remained in his usual seat. The sergeant in the fourth seat down, also at the bar, had apparently either completely forgotten about him or didn't care and just wanted to be left alone.

It was easy back then to feel embarrassed at the sight of these people, and yet, now look at him. *Is this why she told me not to judge?* Wilkinson wondered.

Before him lay 3 empty glasses, and he held a 4th pint of Yuengling in his hand. Wilkinson judged how drunk he was by whether or not he could still tell time. If he could still tell the time compared to actually telling the time, he was not fucking drunk like that funny meme he saw on imgur.com. However, he did notice the lights seemed brighter and all the bottles and their labels appeared shinier as he continued to drink. At least he could still remember his name.

"Hey, green boy, come—*hiccup*—here," someone spoke up from behind him. Wilkinson stood up with his beer in hand and made his way to the seat he'd taken last time he came to the bar. He was stumbling, but managed to still maintain his balance. The sergeant followed him.

"So, what happened?" the sergeant inquired.

"I, I don't know what you mean," Wilkinson slurred. Apparently, he was more drunk than he previously realized.

"You are different, and you not on your partner's leash," the sergeant expressed, trying to rephrase his original question.

"I don't know where she is. I, I haven't seen her since the morning after we had sex," Wilkinson answered. He was sure he hadn't meant to say that; however, this caused both the captain and the sergeant to instantly spit out their mouth fulls of beer.

"Shut the fu–*hiccup*–ck up." The drunk man suddenly perked up, feeling much more alert at the sound of Wilkinson's last statement.

"You mean you slept over and she gave you a morning hug?" the other drunk man from the counter suggested.

"No, I, I passed, passed my lesson on women. My partner took me to Club Pumps. I passed. She, she took me to her place to eat. She, she invited girl from club. They, they danced. Partner picked me up, and they lead me to bedroom," Wilkinson stammered, recalling the events of that night.

"Holy crap! You got the holy grail of sex?" the guy from the counter exclaimed, sounding both impressed and astounded.

"Huh? I don't think I should be telling you this," Wilkinson remarked, sounding confused. "I miss Sarah, she went missing… I could do with a SoCo and Coke."

"I think you've had and said enough. You don't want to make the lady angry now," someone commented from behind, as a hand landed on Wilkinson's right shoulder. Captain Howard nodded to the bartender in acknowledgement.

"Coffee please, and thank you for the call." Howard reached under Wilkinson's arm to help lift him up from his seat, and directed him to another booth, as the sergeant returned to the counter not before the drunk captain stopped him to ask "I bet..*hic-up*..had to ask for directions..haha" he said laughing however the sergeant didn't get to answer

As Wilkinson blurted out "South! Due south of the Alps but, but if you meet any bloody Abrigo-knees you've gone too far south. Bloody Abrigo-knees and their didgeridoos."

"So, how you doing, Wilkinson?" Howard asked, as he sat down opposite Wilkinson to wait for his coffee.

"Captain, when did you get here?" Wilkinson questioned, with a surprised tone in his voice. Apparently, everything that just happened had totally escaped him. The bartender walked over to the table to deliver Howard's coffee.

"Thanks. How many has he had?" Howard requested from the bartender.

"I told him that one was his last – his 9th. He didn't see I was taking the empty glasses away. He came in here about two hours ago, kept saying he went over to her apartment, that he got promoted to red before he started rambling," the bartender reported. "He wasn't driving, else I would have cut him off sooner. I knew he was with Detective Sarah, and I knew Sarah was in your department, so I called you."

"Thanks, I appreciate it," Howard stated, as he handed him a $100 bill.

"Drink it. It's your SoCo you wanted," Howard lied to Wilkinson. Upon hearing this, Wilkinson immediately picked it up to take a sip, but then set the cup back down.

"That's really hot SoCo. Sarah did say whiskey is meant to be drank neat," Wilkinson commented, with a small smile across his face.

"She is a smart lady," Howard laughed. "Drink up, and I'll take you back to your place."

8 CHAPTER EIGHT

Chris woke to an arousing sensation. He thought he knew what was going on, so he kept his eyes closed until he became more awake and aware of his surroundings. He felt the pleasure growing stronger, as he began to understand what was happening more clearly. Chris partially opened one eye to find Courtney lying next to him with her hand under the sheet.

"I see you peeking," Courtney chirped seductively. Chris opened both of his eyes.

"I wasn't too sure if I was dreaming; I didn't want it to end," Chris admitted, as the pleasure continued.

"I'm just inspecting the wood." Courtney winked, as she started to rub harder. "You got to have your fun." A wild smile spread across her face.

"So, what's the plan?" Chris questioned.

"I fancy on taking a ride." She suddenly sat up and straddled Chris, facing him as she slid him inside her. She felt his full firm length inside her, as she started to move her hips back and forth. Her muscles tightened rhythmically, hugging his length, while her hips continued to gyrate. She loved seeing the reaction on Chris's face each time she squeezed tighter.

He made a few attempts to reach up toward her chest; however, Courtney kept his arms down to his sides and swatted his hands away. She was the one in control this time. She continued riding him.

She just had to see the intensity again that he displayed during their first tryst.

She leaned forward and bit into Chris's left shoulder, who had been silent until then, though his facial expression didn't require any subtitles. Once again, as soon as she bit him, Chris started to roar. He instantly enveloped his arms around her, placing one hand behind her head as he thrusted up hard. His hand behind her head prevented her from bending backward, and all in one movement, he had completely flipped her over, so he was now on top. She felt intense pressure against her cervix as he repetitively rammed his length inside her. She wasn't sure if she was afraid of these new sensations, but it felt like everything was inside of her.

"You know we have to pay for the bed if we break it," Courtney commented aloud.

"It will be worth every fucking pound I give you," Chris replied sharply. "I'm going to pound you so hard, there will be an imprint of me inside you forever!"

"I don't think it works like that," she stated with a hint of sarcasm in her voice. Although, for her efforts, she got what she wanted and he started to thrust even harder. He placed a hand around her throat as he held her down against the bed. She tempted fate and tightened her muscles again around his length, which did the trick and sent him over the edge. He rammed deeper and harder inside her, while still pinning her down until he finally exploded inside her for the umpteenth time. Chris collapsed on top of Courtney with his head to the right of hers. She wrapped her arms around him in a hug, as she could hear him panting, trying to catch his breath.

"Right, I'm satisfied now," Courtney giggled. "You okay?"

"How did I get on top?" he asked sounding confused, yet still panting.

"I think you spun us both around. I think we cleared air, or you rolled us when you thrusted into me when I bit into you," she answered, smiling at him. He looked up to see if she was being serious, and then face-planted back into the pillows after realizing her statement was accurate.

"So, what is the plan?" He pushed himself up from the bed, not caring he was completely naked, and sauntered into the bathroom. Knowing she was watching him, he closed the door behind him as he entered the bathroom.

"You know Lynn attempted to reply back to you? There is a missed call from my account on Facebook," Courtney remarked, loud enough for Chris to hear her through the bathroom door.

"There isn't anything we can do about that now. We will have to proceed and tread carefully. If certain people I know find out that you are back in England, they may come to find you, including her mother," Chris hollered back in reply.

"So, let us focus on why I am here, what do you intend to do?" Courtney questioned, as Chris finally returned from the bathroom, still fully naked. She thought about seconds, but it was just about then that the numbness wore off and she started to feel sore, so she resisted and started getting dressed again.

"Well, Raven's dad believes she is staying over with me. He doesn't know she has left the country. She told her sisters and mother, but he was left in the dark," Chris explained.

"Do you have any ideas or suspicions on what he could be doing to her?" Courtney inquired.

"It is something she was afraid to let happen to her sisters. He is a violent man, so I suspect it is something along those lines," Chris continued, as he finished getting dressed and stood up to face Courtney. "I wanted to get you inside the house to her room. He is expecting her back tonight, so I wanted to get you in before he is back, then see what happens."

"What time is it now?" Courtney asked.

"13:00," Chris answered. "He will be back home around 8pm, when it is dark, so we have time."–He walked over and sat on the bed with Courtney–"What is the exit plan?" he questioned.

"I was given two, depending what happens. However, in any event, after we are done, we have to get back to Norwich Airport. Depending what happens once we get there, we will be able to decide what to do next from that point," Courtney explained.

~

In the meantime, nine thousand miles away, the door to Raven's hotel room opened, and Michael and Raven exited the room. Yesterday, they found a care package from Lynn waiting for them in the room. Courtesy of this package, Raven was now decked out in all black clothes, including an HIM t-shirt. Michael was still wearing his same clothes from the prior day.

"We should get a taxi; it will be a mad house to drive back after the concert," Michael suggested.

"Well, we have nothing planned afterwards, so there won't be any rush. Plus, if you drive, we can leave and do whatever we want when we want and won't be restricted. And besides, taxis will overcharge like crazy, I'm sure," Raven replied.

"Alright," he agreed. Michael went back inside to get his car keys, which were laying on one of the nightstands by the bed. He noticed the letter Raven was reading the night before lying on the other nightstand.

"Come on!" Raven shouted. With that, the letter was forgotten as Michael headed back out of the room, keys in hand.

"Do you want to go and eat first?" Michael questioned.

"Have you not gone to a concert before? You should wait until after to eat or eat light. Just drink water, so you don't become dehydrated. Your body doesn't have time to process the food if you eat just before the concert, and when you go to dance, you will make yourself sick," Raven explained.

As they walked down the hallway and passed a mirror, Raven suddenly stopped and noticed her eyeliner was smudged and needed to be fixed. She touched it up with the heavy black eye liner she had on hand.

"I still can't believe Chris got me the tickets. I've wanted to see these guys play for ages," Raven remarked.

"It should be fun," Michael replied, as they continued on toward the car.

"So, are you involved in Lynn's plan too then?" Raven asked.

"What plan?" he responded, sounding puzzled.

"The conspiracy between my boyfriend and Lynn to get me out of the way," she stated.

"What for?" Another perplexed look spread across his face, which Raven could tell was an honest reaction. She took that to mean Michael was simply a pawn in the plan, just like her.

Raven was certainly not pleased by this whole situation, and she felt frustrated as hell that Chris had gone to his old flame for help. However, they'd gone about it the right way, to satisfy her by paying her with clothes and money to have fun. Well, there is nothing to be done. If they wanted to her to have fun, then that was what she was going to do, and Chris wouldn't be able to blame her, as he was the one who sent her here in the first place.

Michael and Raven turned to step into the elevator, so they could ride down to the lobby. The pair looked just like a couple Children of the Night, as the elevator doors slid closed.

9 CHAPTER NINE

Detective Sarah pulled up outside the hospital, just as dusk was quickly approaching. The sun began to sink below the horizon. She turned off the car's engine, and glanced around, being careful to not be seen. She turned the burner cell on again to send a text– *I'm outside.*

She turned the phone back off and continued to wait. Just a few moments later, a tap came on the passenger side window. The door opened and a woman, who Sarah thought had an uncanny resemblance to Halsey climbed into the passenger seat. She had blue hair, and was wearing scrubs with kittens on them. Her badge pinned to her scrubs indicated she was a nurse.

"*Sorry,* do I know you?" Sarah questioned, with a hint of skepticism in her voice.

"No, but I'm a friend of a mutual friend you just texted. They said you need to be at KHPN by 2am. They due to arrive between 2 and 3. Got it?" the nurse remarked.

"2am, KHPN–Got it. Give our friend this box. Tell her to keep it near her, and this one is the one she wanted," Sarah commented, as she handed over the 2 boxes.

"I'm bad at love," the nurse quietly muttered, which made Sarah chuckle softly.

"What?" the nurse responded.

"You have a strong likeness to Halsey, and what you just said didn't help to convince me you are not," Sarah said with a smile.

"Thanks for the compliment," she replied, smiling in return. "She's my lesbian crush. Halsey is amazing."

"Oh, I see. What did you mean though?" Sarah asked. The nurse, Megan, bowed her head down, though Sarah still didn't actually know her name.

"Oh, it's nothing really. Just our friend, for how smart she is, she is really bad at love." She shook her head to release the thought, as she got up and out of the car without another word, leaving Sarah by herself once again. The nurse's words had sparked thoughts of Blue, or now Red, as she had promoted him. She leaned forward to smell the rose she was still wearing. Not wanting to risk being seen any longer, she started the engine and drove off into the night.

~

Courtney, with Chris in the passenger seat, slowly pulled to a stop outside of Raven's dad's home. No one was home right now. It seemed planned, as it was still early on in the day. His woman friend would still be a work. He lived on an estate in Watford, so they didn't risk staying too long and being spotted or considered suspicious.

"So, you don't have any idea what he is doing to her?" Courtney inquired.

"My imagination does, for sure; I'm hoping that it is wrong," Chris replied.

"You really think it is that bad?" she continued. Chris didn't reply, forcing Courtney to accept his silence as a response.

"Still no response from Lynn yet, I hope she got this covered," Chris remarked, abruptly changing the subject. He was still primarily worried about Lynn's mother. He would always see her in town, but didn't really know how to react or what to say to her once she found out that who she thought was her daughter had come back to England and left without saying anything to her.

"I'm going to send her the update notification now. You have an idea where you want to leave the car? It cannot be anywhere in sight of the house, as he may get suspicious," Chris suggested, as he flipped open Messenger under Courtney's Facebook profile name and wrote: *Touring the sights with Lynn having a lovely time, wish you...* He paused for a moment, thinking he could use this to drop a hint since they were told to use code, but would Lynn actually understand? He decided to chance it. He deleted the *wish you* and continued typing again. *I really wish Lynn's mother could be with us too. I'm sure she would have loved to come on the trip too.*

~

Lynn stood by Raven's bedside of Raven while Lola and Ann were still in the thick of playing cards. Lynn looked over the message Chris sent almost a week ago now. Shutting off the phone, she glanced in Raven's direction before turning her attention back to the table.

"Have you made a decision yet?" Lola questioned, watching Lynn as she sat back down.

Just then, the door opened and Megan arrived from outside holding the items that Sarah had given her.

"Your friend said to give you this and to keep it close to you. This box, she said you wanted," Megan reported, as she presented the boxes to Lynn.

"Thanks," Lynn replied gratefully, as she placed both boxes, the one with the lock and the one with the phone, on the floor by her feet. She knew one contained a lock and the other contained a phone.

"What are those?" Lola inquired.

"Insurance," Lynn stated coldly. "I think my initial reaction is the correct one, to answer your original question."

Lynn continued watching Lola, Ann, and Megan play cards. As usual, Lynn was already out, as she still had yet to fully master the art of Texas Hold'em like Lola had.

"Don't worry about it. You can tell me your answer again when you can believe yourself," Lola responded, looking directly at Lynn. She, along with everyone else in the room, could see conflict was waging in Lynn's mind.

"Any update from your puppy?" Lola asked next. However, she never received an answer. Everyone suddenly froze and dropped their cards, as they all slowly turned to look at the bed.

Raven was now awake and had sat up in the bed. Her hair had totally transformed to the blackest of black that reflected absolutely no light. Megan, being more used to this than the others, quickly regained her composure after the initial shock, and instantly got up to tend to Raven. She gently pushed her back down to rest her head on the pillow, so as to avoid dislodging any of the wires and IV tubes connected to her.

"It's okay, Raven. You are in a hospital in New York. You remember what happened to you?" Megan explained, falling into her routine to gauge the extent of any brain damage or memory loss that may have occurred.

"I went inside of the house with Michael. I went down to the basement, as Michael had walked into an argument that was going on with his parents. That is all I remember," Raven said slowly, looking directly at Megan.

Lynn stepped up close behind Megan.

"I'm glad you are awake again. You've had us worried," Lynn remarked.

"Your sister's been here by your side the entire time," Megan inserted, as she prepared to check Raven's temperature.

"She isn't my sister…?" Raven responded, sounding puzzled.

Megan turned toward Lynn with an expression on her face as clear as could be that she wasn't surprised at all.

"Oh really… strange," Megan announced, as more of a statement towards Lynn than a reply to Raven.

"What happened to her hair?" Ann questioned.

"It can happen," Megan started to explain.

"What do you mean?" Raven interrupted. Lynn grabbed a mirror and held it up for Raven to see her reflection, as Raven's hands were still bandaged, thus preventing her from holding anything.

"When your hair dies, it normally goes white; however, it is just a chemical reaction from the soot and ash from the fire. It must've gotten in and mixed into her hair follicles, so as her hair died, it turned black instead of white," Lola reported, finishing Megan's explanation.

"Exactly!" Megan confirmed.

"I love it!" Raven exclaimed.

"We did let Chris know what happened. He is on his way over now," Lynn noted, as she forced a straight face. Lynn was rapidly becoming annoyed by this whole situation. The more time she spent with Raven, the more she actually liked her. She found a lot of things in common between them, like the way she thought. She also liked the puppy, AKA Chris, being in love with her from afar. Then Raven came along and took the puppy away from her. As a result, she wanted to test and punish her.

"*But jealousy, jealousy, jealousy, jealousy*
Get the best of me
Look, I don't mean to frustrate, but I
Always make the same mistakes, yeah I
Always make the same mistakes 'cause
I'm bad at love," Megan sang under her breath.

She watched Lynn as she rolled her eyes. What appeared obvious to her apparently seemed to mystify Lynn.

"Oh, really? He is? Can you finish telling me what happened, Lynn?" Raven requested.

"You heard me?" Lynn quickly turned her attention back to Raven, sounding shocked.

Raven nodded in reply.

"You might as well tell us all now. Would be nice, since you used my store!" Lola insisted.

All the women gathered their chairs they had been using around the table a few moments ago, and pulled them to sit around the bed. Lynn chose to remain standing. It reminded her of story time in preschool. She laughed out loud at the thought.

"Okay, ready children?" Lynn asked of the group. Megan locked the door, so they wouldn't be disturbed. She had placed a nurse placard on the other side of the door, so the other staff members would know not to be worried by a locked door.

"Then I shall continue…" Lynn began, as no one responded to her prior statement.

~

Chris unlocked the back door of Raven's father's house using the key he'd snatched from her back at the airport. Courtney stood rather close behind him, waiting for him to get the door open.

It was approaching 18:00 by their watches. They would have two hours to wait, if he was on time. Once the door was unlocked, Chris let himself into the house, followed by Courtney.

Once inside, they shut the door behind them. They made sure to lock the door, so Raven's father wouldn't suspect anything.

"It's a nice home," Courtney commented, as she looked around the home. "You wouldn't suspect anything just from appearance," she sighed.

"How people like him get away with it. I guess for that very reason. No one suspects, no one wants to think their neighbor could be doing something bad, or no one cares," Chris explained.

"Her room is upstairs," he said, pointing toward the stairs.

Chris opened the door to Raven's room, and put the stuff he brought on the bed. He opened the closet door and checked to make sure he could fit inside with the door at least partially closed, if not completely closed.

"So, the plan is for you to be pretending to be Raven. You be in here waiting for him to arrive, as I will be hiding in the closet. I suggest you be in the bed pretending to be asleep. We should be able to find out what he has been doing to her that way," Chris explained.

"Right, and you will leave him to me, okay? Whatever it is we find out he has been doing, you promise to let me handle it?" Courtney requested. "It's important, Chris. I'm not going to be defenseless," she continued, as she flashed the knife she had with her.

"What about his girlfriend?" Chris questioned.

"If it goes well, nothing. If not, then again, I will deal with it. We have to muddy Lynn's reputation, not yours," Courtney insisted.

"He is not expected back for another two hours, right?" Courtney inquired.

Chris nodded in response.

"I have to get naked anyway to change, right?" she hinted, as she tried to make a playful attempt at sparking his interest.

"No, I love Raven," Chris stated, pushing back.

"That didn't stop you before…" Courtney retorted.

"That was… That was…" Chris began, fumbling for words.

"Because you love Lynn too, and I looked too much like her for you to handle," Courtney interjected, finishing his sentence for him. "Can't you pretend I'm her again?"

"Not in here," he responded, as he knelt down beside the bed. He pulled out the shoe box he knew would be there, which held all the mementos Raven had saved over time. Unbeknownst to both of them, the red light went out on Chris's phone and an incoming FaceTime call appeared on the screen.

"I'll go get changed in the bathroom," Courtney stated forcibly, realizing she had been rejected. She felt defeated in her attempt to seduce Chris; however, it did kind of renew her faith in Chris that he may actually love Raven like he claims. It was obvious though, he was still in love with Lynn too. She could tell by the look on his face when he stumbled to explain why he had slept with her back in the hotel that he was even trying to lie to himself.

Chris answered the FaceTime call. It was Lynn's mom, Mrs. Spoonman.

"Hey, Chris, what you up to?" she asked.

"Nothing, hanging out at Raven's." He thought it'd be simpler to just tell the truth, to a degree.

"Have you spoken to or seen Lynn recently?" she inquired. There it was, the searching question. Chris was stuck on how to answer. He didn't know what he was supposed to say or do.

"Why?" he responded, as that was all he could muster while he tried to think of what to say next.

"Because Facebook is saying you and Lynn are nearby each other, which is odd because you are at Raven's house, right? So, why would Lynn be at Raven's when she should be in New York?" she explained, beginning to sound confused. Chris felt like he was being scolded by a teacher in high school again, and he was angry with himself for not turning off the location on his phone.

Not knowing what else to do, Chris just tapped the "End Call" button and turned off the phone. He felt extremely guilty for betraying Lynn's mother. He liked her and didn't want to see her get hurt.

As soon as he turned his phone off, Courtney's phone started to get messages from Courtney's Facebook profile, meaning they were from Lynn.

The coded message read: *Hey, Chris, it was great to hear about the trip. I'm sure Lynn is missing her mother too. She was made aware of the trip before it started, she just couldn't make it on time.*

How did she know he turned off his phone? Chris thought. He turned it back on and messaged Courtney's Facebook account. *Everything is going as planned. She is getting changed.*

Is there something you would like to say to Lynn? Or Raven perhaps? She is having lots of fun with Michael. They staying together tonight in a hotel. They be going to the HIM concert as planned. Lynn sent a message back to Chris. She wanted to give him the chance to say something. She didn't know what she wanted him to say or why she was trying to mess with Chris's head by telling him about Raven and Michael.

Please tell Raven, I miss her a lot. …and yes, but it wouldn't do any good. She is here to help me, help Raven. Chris held an old picture of himself with an old letter he had written to Raven, as he typed a response.

Lynn rolled her eyes. *When will boys realize if girls are asking, then they already know?* she wondered, as she sighed. Lynn looked at her watch and saw it was almost time to head to the Credo's store to start setting everything up. So be it, she decided.

"He's picked his course," she muttered to herself as she prepared to message him one more time.

Make sure Lynn leaves gifts before returning. She should leave gifts of herself in Raven's bed. Do. Not. Anger, Lynn. She should get to leave some gifts of the trip. There. Lynn sent her cryptic response.

"Courtney should get to enjoy herself as well… one last time," Lynn commented under her breath, shrugging.

"What did she mean by that?" Chris wondered aloud.

"She is telling you to have sex with me," Courtney chimed from the doorway, where she stood completely naked. He hadn't notice she had returned. "You see the capital letters? D, N, A? I need to leave DNA in the bed, so they know Lynn was here and not Raven. I could leave hair and skin, but nothing works better than the juices of a woman." She knelt down and pulled him up by his hand.

"It's okay, I know you love Raven… and Lynn, but this was always part of the plan. When they find him dead, do you want them to think Raven did this or you? Of course not. It is better they think it is Lynn and confuse them.

While they are sorting out the confusion, Lynn will be able to prove she was in America the entire time. By the time they sort out the mess, we will be gone and they will not have any leads, but more importantly Raven will not be implicated, so don't feel bad," she explained, as she undid the button on his pants and forced them to the ground.

"You, by having sex with me again, will be protecting Raven. You've been with her before here, so it will be only natural your DNA will be here and they will assume it was a cross contamination."

Chris was still not one hundred percent certain; however, reason and logic were slipping away quickly, as a naked woman stood in front of him while his pants were down around his ankles.

Courtney walked up to him and kissed him. Knowing what she needed to do, she slowly started to kiss the right side of Chris's neck. A tingling sensation flooded through his body. He instantly developed a full erection extending even beyond his foreskin.

"Drill me," she whispered in his ear, as she felt the success of her efforts to seduce him.

She took advantage of Chris's weakness and bit into his neck. Chris instantly transformed into his animalistic state of passion. He roared, as he picked her up and forced her onto the bed. She was half on the bed and half off with her legs in the air wrapping around his neck. He leaned forward over her, and began to thrust his length inside her.

"What you waiting for? I want to see your signature move–drill me," she coaxed.

Using nothing but his closed fists to support himself, he continued to thrust hard and fast. If you blinked, you would have missed nearly 6 thrusts. He moved like a jackhammer, hence the term "drilling". He used the recoil of the bed to counter each thrust, so as to avoid needing to pull back and thus allowing him to keep pounding faster and faster.

Courtney reached over to grab a pillow and stuff it into her mouth to keep her from screaming at the top of her lungs and alerting the neighbors that someone was home. The pillow stifled some of her moans, but not by much. She felt her insides being destroyed, as he continued to do as he was commanded.

She was slowly becoming paralyzed with each recurrent thrust. Significant pain mixed with equal amounts of pleasure until everything just felt numb inside her. As the pain dissolved, she allowed him to continue pushing through that wall. Eventually, her phone alarm went off, alerting they only had 1 hour before Raven's father was expected home. She reached up around his neck and pulled him in close, nothing else would have gotten through to him.

"Cum now. Finish me," she ordered, breathlessly. She was breathing heavily with her mouth hanging open. One final thrust all the way made her truly believe he had completely battered her cervix with the full force of his erect length being used as the battering ram. It certainly felt like it, even though she knew that wasn't really possible. It did the trick though. As soon as she pushed him off, everything started to flow out of her. She made certain a mixture of him and her coated the bed.

Now, all that was left, was for her to get into position and wait, though she didn't relish the thought. She laid in the bed and pretended to be asleep, while Chris hid in the closet.

~

Wilkinson, or Red, woke up with the worst headache he could have ever imagined. Despite his blurry vision, he saw someone place a Yankees mug in front of him.

"Drink it, it's coffee," Captain Howard ordered. "Don't do the drink, if you can't pay the bill," he remarked sternly.

Wilkinson didn't respond, but sat up and started to sip the very strong black coffee.

"We may just Americanize you yet, Wilkinson," the Captain commented, as he notice Red drinking the coffee without spitting it out or making a strange facial expression despite the strong bitter taste.

"Now, explain what is going on with you. I got the gist of it last night. You do know, because a women sleeps with you doesn't always mean they have to love you? Certainly not from what you describe," Howard stated.

"How come you are not talking like she is dead, like everyone else?" Wilkinson questioned.

"I didn't know for sure until I saw you last night. I've seen people fall head first into drink before. It is always because of a woman. She's done a number on you, hasn't she? Meaning, you saw or found something and you didn't know how to handle it," he sighed. "So, explain."

"It's slightly embarrassing," Wilkinson began.

"It often is… Don't let that stop you now," Howard coached.

"My partner was teaching me to understand women, to be better able to go after my perp, as I never had a relationship. I wasn't a virgin, except the only experience I had was one I paid for. She took me to Ferrell's to get the male perspective on women. Sarah said drunk people tell no lies."

"She isn't kidding," Howard quipped. "Go on."

"The whole thing with the club she setup, so she could deal with her case and help me with what she called my education. The guys at Ferrell's asked me *if I really hadn't thought about being with Sarah*," Wilkinson remembered. "I didn't know what they meant by that. To me, she was just my partner."

"The club, I saw, I really saw for the first time, as if I had my eyes open for the first time. A place like that, where I always believed degraded or belittled women, when in fact the total opposite is true. They are in total control of you. Soon as you walk in, they have you hooked mind and body. They can twist you and manipulate you, and we are dumb enough to let them. It is a perfect example of how strong and intelligent women can really be.

"However, it was there she had opened my eyes. I didn't even know it was her at first. I saw how she commanded the room she passed through. She was able to have everything sorted and setup with her plan. She also dealt with the surprise of Lynn showing up, and still found time to educate me and help me get my first arrest. She did it all while looking perfectly stunning."

"She is a strong woman with confidence, like your perp. You will find confidence is the key to a lot of things like that," Howard noted.

"I went back to her apartment earlier to see if she saw the flowers I left for her," he added quietly.

"Oh, God, you didn't just fall. You tripped over the edge of the summit off the high mountain and fell 600ft straight down for her, haven't you?!" Howard exclaimed, chuckling.

"Wouldn't you? For a woman who gave you–what did the guys call it? The holy grail of sex?" Wilkinson posed. "However, when I went back tonight, she'd written a response on the back of the card. How could she do that if she is dead?" He handed the message card over to his Captain.

"It's the club all over again! She is setting something up, I just don't understand what!" Wilkinson explained.

"You may have to accept it isn't," Howard stated solemnly. "When she came to speak to me alone after your debrief, she told me Lynn spoke to her as she was leaving the club. Lynn told her she was on the wrong side. She told me she was not inclined to help her… but if she isn't dead and just in the dark…?"

"Never… She wouldn't have reached out to me like this." Wilkinson held up the card, as he interrupted in protest.

"She left you saying she knew where Lynn was with the phone, which had everything on it, vanishes when the call went out about Credo's murder…" Howard paused for a moment. Mrs. Howard wasn't exactly the most loyal wife to him, but he had still cared for her. It was still disconcerting for him to refer to his wife's murder as 'the Credo's murder'.

"Her car was found at the house that exploded with no trace. She either has gone over or Lynn has something on her, which would be a good reason to make everyone think she is dead.

"We need to do something to help her out of whatever mess she is in now!" Howard exclaimed, as he paced the floor impatiently.

This, of all things, sparked a memory of Wilkinson's when he said something similar.

"Relax, Blue, you can't rush a girl. She will come out of the bathroom when she is good and ready in about 5 minutes," Wilkinson recited aloud.

"Where can I enroll in that University of Sarah?" Howard joked. He smiled somewhat sympathetically, though Blue's point did hit home.

Red's phone buzzed, notifying him he had a text. He picked it up and saw it came from a blocked number. It simply read: *KHPN*.

~

"I've missed your calls for months it seems
Don't realize how mean I can be
'Cause I can sometimes treat the people
That I love like jewelry
'Cause I can change my mind each day
I didn't mean to try you on
But I still know your birthday
And your mother's favorite song," Sarah quietly sang to herself, as she turned the burner cell back off and continued driving toward her destination.

~

Courtney was in place, lying in the bed. Chris checked the list of instructions saved on his phone. Lynn had saved this same list onto Courtney's phone so many days earlier while she was still back in America. Chris propped Courtney's phone up against the window, with the camera facing the window. The main screen faced into the room from behind the light cloth sheers covering the window. He didn't pull the curtains closed.

"You okay? We still have time to pull out of this," Chris suggested, watching Courtney's nervous expression.

"Mhmm," she nodded. "I'm determined. I know what it is like being controlled. He deserves what's coming to him."

~

"Wait, you had him set up a phone?" Raven asked, sounding sort of surprised. Although, it was impossible to fully identify what, if any, emotion Raven was expressing. Lynn nodded in response.

"I want to see it," Raven insisted.

"I don't think that is such a …," Lynn started to say.

"LET ME SEE IT !" Raven demanded, nearly yelling. Lynn glanced towards Lola and Megan, who both nodded in return.

"Can one of you get my spare phone from the bag on my chair please? It's Android, not the iPhone," Lynn requested. It was the fastest request ever met as Ann had leapt up from her chair, grabbed the bag, and passed it to Lynn. She retrieved the phone with the recording.

"So I'm sorry to my unknown lover
Sorry that I can't believe
That anybody ever really
Starts to fall in love with me
Sorry to my unknown lover
Sorry I could be so blind
Didn't mean to leave you
And all of the things that we had behind," Megan chimed softly, as she waited for Lynn to find the video.

They all went around the other side of the bed. Lynn held the phone where everyone could see, and played the video.

~

Red and Captain Howard were rampant, bursting out of the apartment. All thoughts of Red's hangover were gone, as they headed down to Howard's car.
"We can't really call for back-up until we know what is going on," Howard shouted.

At the same time, Lynn, Lola, and Megan had staged a little hospital break for Raven. Megan was driving her truck, while the others were piled into the passenger seats. Lola sat in the front passenger seat, while Lynn sat stuck between Raven and Ann across the rear bench seat. They were crossing over the bridge to head into Manhattan. Raven's skin had largely turned black as a result of the explosion, which matched the black outfit she was wearing, the same outfit she'd worn the day of the concert. She sat mostly silent with the phone on her lap paused on the video.

"Your father used to assault you, didn't he?" Lynn asked softly. No one said a word. During the initial viewing, Raven had snatched the phone, paused it, and demanded to meet them when they arrived. Despite all their protests, no one really wanted to stand in her way. Lynn knew all too well that nothing was going to stop her, even if she had to crawl all the way to the airport, so she gave in and just helped her get dressed.

Now, she just sat silent in the car, tears streaming from her eyes, with the image paused.

"I run away when things are good
And never really understood
The way you laid your eyes on me
In ways that no one ever could
And so it seems I broke your heart
My ignorance has struck again
I failed to see it from the start
And tore you open 'til the end," Megan sang under her breath once again. Lola noticed and lifted one eye to glance at Megan, but she still refrained from saying anything.

Sarah pulled through the General Aviation (GA) entrance to the airport. She pulled up the flight plan that had been filed for their flight, as she made her way to park near the tie down for the aircraft and waited. It was only 01:50, still 10 minutes to go. The truck carrying the 4 other women entered through the same entrance and parked close to Sarah's car.

Lynn, Lola, and Ann got out of the truck and walked over to Sarah. Megan just sat there motionless and silent, as she watched Raven through the rearview mirror. Raven was slightly crying, as she continue to stare at the frozen image on the phone.

Raven felt as though she was the only person in the world, and all that mattered was the phone in her hands. Everything else around her was just white noise.

Finally, Raven moved the slider back to the start and hit play again.

~

The room was blacked out, while Chris continued to wait in the closet. He didn't risk turning on his phone to check the time, but each passing second felt like ages. He made a couple of attempts to make sure Courtney was not actually sleeping, but she just kept shushing him in response to his efforts.

All traces of light outside were long gone now as well, which made the room appear even darker. It would have been pitch black, had it not been for an amber street lamp shining some light into the room. Neither Chris nor Courtney could hear anything from downstairs, but they knew his woman friend had to be home by that point. Finally, they started to hear a heavily intoxicated man stumble up to the door, yelling and cursing, as he fumbled with keys trying to unlock the door into the house. He eventually made his way inside the house.

"O'ey, you home?! Hey! You home yet?!" the man shouted at the top of his lungs. They could hear loud thumping sounds, which Chris assumed was from him removing his boots, followed by heavy footsteps coming up the stairs.

"Hey, don't ignore me you ungrateful cunt! Without me, you're nothing!" The door flew open, and his silhouette appeared in the doorway.

"HEY!" he roared as loud as he could. "Don't you dare ignore me, I'll teach you better, bitch!"

Chris was already at the limits of his patience, of what he could tolerate. Chris heard Raven's father remove his belt, and before Chris could fully comprehend what was happening, Raven's father had pulled the belt tight with his right hand and let go. The belt buckle struck the girl in bed, who he thought was his daughter, causing a huge gash in her forehead.

Courtney gasped and cried out in pain, reacting to the belt slamming into her head. Raven's father noticed the voice didn't sound like Raven, even in the dark and in his drunken state. He flipped the room's light on with his right hand. That was it for Chris. Seeing Raven's father in the light with his pants around his ankles and having witnessed what he just did was all he could handle. Chris felt enraged. He let out a war cry of sorts, burst out of the closet, and launched himself up onto Raven's father's back.

"NOOOO!!!" Courtney screamed, as she immediately stretched out a hand, wanting to stop Chris, but she had reacted too slow. It was too late. The light brought to life his worst imagination. Red filled their vision, as Chris's cries and declaration of love for Raven echoed throughout the house, while blood from Raven's father's throat splattered onto Courtney and all over the room. Chris had slit his throat, leaving no time for him to react. An expression of shock still covered his face, as the life drained from his eyes.

~

Raven rewound the video again just enough to see the moment again where Chris busted out of the closet, bringing fresh tears to Raven's eyes.

"So I'm sorry to my unknown lover
Sorry that I can't believe
That anybody ever really
Starts to fall in love with me
Sorry to my unknown lover
Sorry I could be so blind
Didn't mean to leave you
And all of the things that we had behind," Megan continued to sing to herself.

"Hey, Sarah, all going okay?" Lynn questioned, as she walked up to her. "Raven woke up sooner than expected. She insisted to see him, so here we are."

"Everything okay?" Lynn asked, as she noticed the rose Sarah had with her.

"Yeah, all is going as planned. I filed with the eAPIS [the Electronic Advance Passenger Information System] and got their confirmation an hour before their crossing into the US. They shouldn't be too far out now."

"My friend loves you, you know?" Lynn commented. "You sure everything is going okay?"

"Lynn, tell us what happened after, please!" Ann interrupted, begging for the conclusion. Lola and Ann had been forced to wait to learn the end of the story, as Raven had paused the video and demanded to come here. Now that they were there, they wanted to know the remainder of the night's events.

~

"Is it a bad trip?" Lynn's voice echoed from the phone Courtney held in her hand, as she stood there still bleeding and staring at Chris. He was frozen in place, having not moved a single step from where he had landed after Raven's father collapsed to the ground beneath him. Chris was only barely aware of what was happening around him, let alone Courtney's phone conversation.

"May have to bring him back home for a time out." The call ended and almost instantly after there was a loud knock on the front door.

"Let me in," a woman's voice sounded with a hushed, yet urgent tone. "It's okay, it's me–Mrs. Spoonman, Lynn's mum!"–she knocked insistently– "Courtney, let me in!"

This sparked Courtney to move, as she darted down the stairs and opened the front door. She rapidly closed it back behind Mrs. Spoonman, and bolted the door shut. She noticed she was leaving bloody handprints on the white back of the front door.

"Where is he?" Mrs. Spoonman questioned impatiently. She quickly looked to Courtney for a response, but when Courtney did not immediately respond, she ran past her and up the stairs. She marched straight into Raven's bedroom and pulled Chris into a tight hug.

"It's okay. You did good." Mrs. Spoonman still remembered when Chris and her son, John, would play together in the pit as kids. this man was playing with her son John in the pit as kids. She released him and stepped back, but then slapped him hard.

"Come on, get it together now," she ordered, trying to spark some life back into Chris.

Being careful not to step in the blood that had drained from Raven's father body, she walked straight over to the window and grabbed the camera. She avoided touching the knife Chris had used.

"Do you still have your knife?" Mrs. Spoonman asked Courtney. "Give it to me," she demanded, as Courtney displayed the knife. "Stay here!" she told Courtney, as she began to escort Chris toward the top of the stairs.

"Go down and out the back. Lorraine is waiting outside," Mrs. Spoonman instructed.

"Lorraine?" Chris asked, sounding completely flummoxed. It had been ages since the last time he saw her.

"Yeah, I had to make sure they didn't do anything foolish soon as they saw 'Lynn' was coming back. When I explained you were in trouble, she didn't hesitate. Now, go!" she directed.

Mrs. Spoonman watched Chris make his way down the stairs, as he obeyed her instruction. She turned back around to return to Raven's bedroom and found Courtney standing there, still looking worried.

"You did a good job," Mrs. Spoonman stated with a smile, as she waved for Courtney to join her. Courtney had just approached Mrs. Spoonman's back, when she suddenly wheeled around to her left and stabbed Courtney in the lower abdomen.

"Steady now. We don't want you to bleed out too quickly," Mrs. Spoonman coaxed. Courtney's initial reaction had been to pull back and pull the blade out of her stomach. Mrs. Spoonman simply stood there, staring at her, as she collapsed to the ground on her back.

"Lynn thanks you for being such a *loyal* friend; however, I am afraid a short few moments ago, your family was just killed in an apparent oil explosion, which Raven set off. Lynn wanted this to look like revenge gone bad. Raven killed your family, so naturally you wanted to strike back. Chris killing him has complicated things, but that cannot be helped now. Chris is kind of like your dad; he cheated on your mom with Lynn," Mrs. Spoonman taunted, as she held up a picture of Lynn and Courtney's dad together.

Courtney could not find her voice to respond, and was just forced to watch and listen. Mrs. Spoonman looked at the time on her phone.

"Well, I must be going. I have to get him out of here now," Mrs. Spoonman added nonchalantly.

She started to slowly pull the knife out, so as to not agitate the wound any further. She aimed to leave a steady flow of blood pumping out onto the floor. Mrs. Spoonman held the knife right in front of Courtney's eyes. She held onto the knife's handle with her tips of her fingers, as she wiped it clean with a Lysol wipe. Once clean, she placed it Raven's father's hand.

Now, the scene would look exactly as Lynn had planned. It appeared that Courtney decided to kill Raven's father after finding out about her family, but she wasn't quick enough and he stabbed her before she managed to slit his throat. Mrs. Spoonman stood up straight, and carefully exited the room, making sure not to touch anything else on her way out and leaving Courtney to slowly bleed out to her death.

~

"Brilliant," Sarah remarked aloud. "They are also going to assume she was trying to discredit you by looking like you, which brings into question all the other crimes they believe you did when you were back in England, as it could have been her the entire time. Of course, it wasn't, but they have no way to know that, so that means they'll recall Red back home," Sarah reported, detailing the ruse. Her voice trailed off, as she began to realize the impact this new development would have. Sarah stood up and locked eyes with Lynn.

"Let me go back to him, please?" she requested.

"You love him too?" Lynn responded, sounding surprised.

"He was just ignorant before. I've been teaching him, improving his knowledge on women. He really isn't the type you are fighting against. He just didn't understand you, and I never met someone that was more deserving of the type of night Chenelle and I gave him, and well… it is just… he gave me flowers after sex."

"Oh wow," Lola and Ann both gasped at the same time.

"And the card he left me–he was concerned about me more than anything," Sarah continued, as she smelled her rose. "I really don't think he cares about catching you anymore. My friends at Ferrell's told me he was a complete train wreck. I've never had someone fall to pieces over me before," Sarah explained.

The noise of a small Cessna 210 plane broke the tension. The noise signaled that they were about to arrive. Raven finally exited the truck, followed by Megan. Raven, with her natural likeness to black, now resonated even more with her avian namesake, as she placed her black fedora on her head and black framed glasses on her face. She had thick black hair, burned and blackened skin, and wore black torn clothes too.

Raven walked over to stand by the others, and Megan followed closely behind her. Megan, still in nurse mode, kept an eye on her, as she ought to still be in bed. She was sure there would be hell to pay if she ever returned to the hospital. However, she didn't care. She wouldn't have missed any of this for the world. Once she reached the group, she stood next to Lola.

"Cold, isn't it? Do you have gloves?" Lola questioned.

Megan put her hands in her pockets in search of gloves, but realized she never had gloves with her, as she was still in her scrubs. Although, what she did find were the two Azure black nail polishes.

"You probably won't have a job after this, and you've more than earned your share," Lola commented, as she began explaining the value of those nail polishes to Megan. Each bottle in her hand was worth over $250,000.00.

The Cessna taxied off the runway after Mrs. Spoonman brought it down for a perfect landing. Seeing all the people, she stopped short of the tie down point. As the props came to a stop, the doors opened.

Lorraine, Mrs. Spoonman, and lastly, Chris, all exited the plane.

Raven pushed past Megan and the others, as she ran straight towards Chris.

"Sorry to my unknown lover
Sorry that I can't believe
That anybody ever really
Starts to fall in love with me
Sorry to my unknown lover
Sorry I could be so blind
Didn't mean to leave you
And all of the things that we had behind," Megan sang quietly. All the women followed suit and joined her in unison.

Raven enveloped Chris in her arms, almost knocking him over. She was a complete mess of emotion, and unable to speak. Lorraine and Mrs. Spoonman smiled at their reunion. Not wanting to intrude, they headed over to join the group.

"We need to get going before Customs gets here," Lynn's mom stated. "We didn't land at port of entry; they will be here soon. I was squawking 7600, faking radio failure," she explained, as she gave Lynn a warm hug.

"In a moment, Mum. I have to finish my plan"–she turned to Lola–"I've made my decision." Lynn then turned to face Sarah again.

"You sure you want him? You want to do this?" Lynn questioned. She received a nod in response. Suddenly, there was a flash of light and a piercing bang echoed through the area, as a shot rung out from the small 6 piece Sarah had given Lynn earlier. Sarah instantly collapsed in a heap on the ground as the bullet fired into Sarah's hip.

Lynn slowly started to walk towards the couple everyone was letting have privacy.

"You bloody fool! Bloody, bloody, bloody fool!" Raven hugged him again. Chris didn't say anything, and just let her do whatever she wanted. He knew it was coming.

Raven grabbed his face and kissed him once passionately. As she broke away from the kiss, she started to finish the song she heard Megan singing.

"Someone will love you
Someone will love you
But someone isn't me," Raven sang slowly. As she finished the tune, she thrust upward, stabbing Chris with a medical scalpel she had taken from Megan.

"You broke your promise to me," she remarked, as she sniffed and wiped her eyes with her sleeve.

Lynn had walked up to join them, and didn't appear surprised at all by what Raven had just done. In fact, she was kind of proud of Raven. Lynn stepped up to Chris as well, and intensely kissed him herself.

"Someone will love you
Someone will love you
But someone isn't me," Lynn sang quietly, and just like Raven had done, she too stabbed Chris as she finished the song. He fell to the ground, clutching his stomach. Lynn stepped back, and stood shoulder to shoulder with Raven.

"She never slept with Michael. But thank you for making Courtney's death meaningless," Lynn commented to Chris, as he laid there on the ground.

As it started to pour down rain, Raven dropped the phone on the ground beside Chris with the video still paused on the image of him slicing her dad's throat.

~

"Hurry!" Red screamed. His phone alerted him to an incoming text.

"Going as fast as I can! We were 2 minutes out," Howard shouted in response.

Red opened the text from the blocked number. "*You better hurry if you want to save her. If you have time, you may be able to save one, but not both. You could decide to come after me, but then no one will be saved*," Red read the text aloud.

The tires screeched as they drifted around the corner, burning rubber on the road. Howard's truck came busting through the gate with lights flashing and sirens blaring. They saw the women climbing into the truck, as Howard stopped the car. Red instantly spotted Lynn as he jumped out of the car. She waved from the truck, as the women started to drive away into the night.

Red instantly ran to Sarah's side. Howard called a 10-33 (emergency and officer in need of assistance) and a 10-52 (ambulance needed) x2 on his radio. As the rain continued to pour down, Howard ran to where Chris laid to start CPR while they waited for the ambulances.

10 CHAPTER TEN

Red is left with a terrible decision to make – save the woman he loves, save Chris, or go after Lynn. What would you decide?

You don't know which to pick?

… *She Knows*!

BE YOUR OWN KIND OF BEAUTIFUL.

There's nothing more dangerous than a woman who knows she is beautiful, and who is focused and unimpressed…

This is not the end for Lynn.